Please return/renew this item by the
last date shown to avoid a charge.
Books may also be renewed by phone
and Internet. May not be renewed if
required by another reader.

www.libraries.barnet.gov.uk

BARNET
LONDON BOROUGH

RISING ★ STARS

Hachette UK's policy is to use papers that are natural, renewable and recyclable products and made from wood grown in well-managed forests and other controlled sources. The logging and manufacturing processes are expected to conform to the environmental regulations of the country of origin.

ISBN: 9781398324305

Text © Adam and Charlotte Guillain
Illustrations, design and layout © Hodder and Stoughton Ltd
First published in 2022 by Hodder & Stoughton Limited (for its Rising Stars imprint, part of the Hodder Education Group),
An Hachette UK Company
Carmelite House 50 Victoria Embankment London EC4Y 0DZ
www.risingstars-uk.com

Impression number 10 9 8 7 6 5 4 3 2 1
Year 2026 2025 2024 2023 2022

Author: Adam and Charlotte Guillain
Series Editor: Tony Bradman
Commissioning Editor: Hamish Baxter
Illustrator: Katie Kear/Bright International Group
Educational Reviewer: Helen Marron
Design concept: David Bates
Page layouts: Rocket Design (East Anglia) Ltd
Editor: Amy Tyrer

With thanks to the schools that took part in the development of *Reading Planet* KS2, including: Ancaster CE Primary School, Ancaster; Downsway Primary School, Reading; Ferry Lane Primary School, London; Foxborough Primary School, Slough; Griffin Park Primary School, Blackburn; St Barnabas CE First & Middle School, Pershore; Tranmoor Primary School, Doncaster; and Wilton CE Primary School, Wilton.

A catalogue record for this title is available from the British Library.

Printed in the United Kingdom

Orders: Please contact Hachette UK Distribution, Hely Hutchinson Centre, Milton Road, Didcot, Oxfordshire, OX11 7HH.

Telephone: (44) 01235 400555. Email: primary@hachette.co.uk.

MIX
Paper from
responsible sources
FSC™ C104740

Contents

1 First Day Back

It was the first day back at school after the summer holidays. As Carter hurried up the hill, the streets were already full of adults and little kids in pushchairs heading away from Greenwicks Primary.

"What's with the face?" said Ryan when he bumped into Carter.

Carter and Ryan had been friends since the first day of pre-school.

"Have you seen my trousers?" said Carter. They were flapping high above his ankles.

Carter had grown quite a bit over the summer. But with everything that had happened, nobody had remembered to buy him a new school uniform.

"Nice socks though," Ryan laughed. "But I don't think Mrs Wilde's going to like those trainers."

It was well known that the headteacher didn't like bright yellow Bart Simpson socks or branded trainers. She liked white socks and black shoes that made running down the corridor almost impossible without slipping over.

Carter felt better walking alongside Ryan. It stopped him thinking about how his dad had packed an overnight bag last night and gone to stay at the hotel up the street.

"I love you, son," Dad had said as he gave Carter the longest hug. Carter had tried hard not to cry, but he had. Why couldn't his parents just make up, like he always had to do with his little brothers?

Carter and Ryan arrived at school late, and had to go through the main entrance instead of heading straight to their class.

"Welcome back," said Mrs Wilde, greeting Carter and Ryan as they signed in. "But let's try and get to school on time tomorrow, please. Year 6 pupils need to set an example. This time next year, you'll be at secondary school and this kind of timekeeping just won't do."

Secondary school? Carter had always felt like he'd be at primary school forever. He definitely didn't feel ready for more change. Still, he had Year 6 to get through first.

By the time Carter and Ryan got to the Year 6 classroom, everyone was already busy reading.

"Carter and Ryan, isn't it?" said their new teacher, Mr Ali. "Welcome to Year 6." He continued, "Carter, your reading group is already in the library choosing books. Ryan, your group is over there by the window."

Carter and Ryan stared at each other.

"But I'm always in a reading group with Ryan," Carter protested.

Ryan looked at their teacher and nodded. "Seriously, Mr Ali, he is," he said. "Since Year 1."

Mr Ali smiled. "Don't worry, you can see each other later. I've just mixed things up a bit this year. Carter, make your way down to the library now and I'll join you as soon as I can."

Carter stomped out of the classroom and barged down the corridor towards the library. This kind of behaviour would have made his previous teachers come after him to 'have a word', so Carter was surprised when he didn't hear Mr Ali's footsteps behind him.

Carter's heart sank when he found his new reading group sitting on the green beanbags in the far corner of the library. He wasn't friends with any of these people. There was Femi, the quiet boy who never played football, and two girls, Lexi and Sara. Carter didn't mind Lexi because she was always in trouble for clowning around and making everyone laugh, but he didn't really know Sara.

Sara had started wearing a hijab over the holidays and was showing Lexi how she wrapped it in a way that stopped it slipping off.

Sara looked up and smiled at Carter. He crashed down on to the nearest beanbag and glared at them.

"How was your summer, Carter?" Sara asked.

"Pretty rubbish," he mumbled.

Carter started banging the heels of his trainers into the carpet. For a few awkward moments it was the only sound in the room.

"Well, welcome to Year 6!" Sara burst out loudly, doing an impersonation of Mr Ali. It made Carter smile, though he didn't really want to.

Then everyone went quiet as a face popped up over the bookshelf.

"You must be Mr Ali's reading group," said Mrs Warner, the librarian. "Do you want to start choosing your books?"

Carter and the two girls got up. Femi was obviously dreaming about something far more interesting and continued gazing into space.

Carter was soon staring at a bookcase, his mind lost in his own story. The one where his mum and dad had been arguing all summer. It made Carter's stomach hurt just thinking about it. Was Dad really going to leave? Would Carter go with him or stay with his mum and little brothers? How was he supposed to choose?

Carter tried to shift his mood by closing his eyes and remembering the song he'd been listening to with his dad. It was called *After the Storm*. Carter loved it – especially the words.

During one of his parents' arguments, Carter had turned the song up really loud and sung along. Carter found that if he really listened, the song blocked out his bad feelings, at least for a few minutes.

Now Carter tapped his hands on the top of the shelf and began to murmur the words again.

"Carter?" asked a voice.

Carter opened his eyes and got ready to be told off.

Instead, he was surprised to see Mr Ali looking at him with a smile on his face.

"What song are you singing?" Mr Ali asked.

"You wouldn't know it," said Carter, shoving his hands into his pockets.

"Maybe not, but I am interested," said Mr Ali.

Carter mumbled the name of the song. Then he watched with raised eyebrows as Mr Ali got some paper to write it down.

"If you're interested in music then we might find a book you'd like here," said Mr Ali, heading to the non-fiction section.

This felt more normal to Carter. Mr Ali was just doing one of those teacher tricks to get him interested in reading.

Mr Ali showed Carter some books that actually looked quite interesting. He picked one and sat down next to Femi.

"Ten more minutes' reading time," Mr Ali announced as he opened the door to leave. "Enjoy it!"

Carter realised Femi was looking at him as he opened his book.

"Mr Ali seems okay, doesn't he?" said Femi quietly.

It was the first time Femi had ever spoken to Carter.

"Yeah," he said. "He's okay."

At that moment, 'okay' felt as good as this awful week was going to get. If his mum and dad really were splitting up, what would it mean? Was Dad going to move far away?

Would Carter have to change schools even before going to secondary school? Everything felt up in the air and not in a good way.

"I think it's pretty cool our group is first to hang out in the library," said Lexi, coming over. "I mean, we're not exactly the star readers, are we?"

"Most teachers wouldn't trust some of us to behave in here," said Sara, smiling.

Carter agreed. Normally he'd have been in trouble about three times by now. If he hadn't been so stressed about the thought of his dad moving out, hanging out with Femi, Lexi and Sara might have made the start of his first day in Year 6 feel all right.

2 A New Club

For the rest of that morning, Mr Ali kept the class working in their reading groups. The topic was 'aspirations'. Mr Ali asked them to talk about the things they wanted to achieve in their last year of primary school.

"I just want to have fun before I go to secondary school and have to do lots of proper work," said Lexi, making the class laugh.

"I don't even want to think about secondary school," said Sara. "Those kids are just too big and scary-looking."

Carter looked up. He was supposed to be going to Rosedale Secondary School.

That's if he stayed here with his mum. None of his friends knew where they were going yet. Would the whole class be split up?

"But what do you want to achieve in the time you have left?" said Mr Ali. "Anyone?"

Carter hunched over the table. While the others started answering Mr Ali's question, all he could think about was his mum and dad.

"Carter, what are your aspirations for this term?" Mr Ali asked walking over to their table.

"Dunno," he mumbled. Carter usually had lots to say, even when he wasn't asked. But not today. Carter felt a bit embarrassed, so he added, "New trousers."

The group laughed but Mr Ali looked thoughtful.

"We'll work on it," he said.

"*What*?!" exclaimed Lexi. "We're going to work on Carter's trousers?"

Everyone laughed again, including Mr Ali.

"We'll work on everything!" said Mr Ali, moving on to the next group.

"You usually get told off when you're cheeky like that," Sara said to Lexi.

Lexi frowned. "But I wasn't trying to be cheeky," she said. "I just thought talking about Carter's trousers was funny!"

Carter was also surprised Mr Ali hadn't told them off. Usually everything he said annoyed his teachers.

Carter always played football with Ryan at lunchtime, but today Carter saw him laughing with Ethan and Sol from his new reading group. Carter looked around the playground for someone else and saw Femi peering through the window into the hall.

He wandered over and was surprised to see Mr Ali sitting at the piano in the hall.

"He's singing," said Femi softly.

Carter strained his ears to hear.

"I think he's writing a song," said Femi.

"How do you know?" asked Carter.

"He keeps stopping to write things down," Femi explained.

Carter had never seen anyone write a song before. He wondered if Mr Ali liked music as much as he and his dad did.

"Let's go in and listen," he said.

But pupils weren't allowed inside at lunchtime. Not without a good reason.

"We'll have to sneak in really quietly so nobody notices," Femi whispered.

But Carter had another idea.

"Mr Ali!" Carter shouted, banging on the window. "Can we come in and listen?"

Carter's banging was so loud Sara and Lexi heard it and came running over. It worked on Mr Ali, too.

"Can we listen to your song?" Carter asked when Mr Ali opened the emergency exit and stepped out.

Mr Ali looked a bit unsure.

"It's allowed," said Lexi with a grin, giving Sara a nudge.

"It is," Sara echoed, her eyes wide and pleading.

Mr Ali said, "I don't see why not," and ushered them in. He let the children pull up a bench and listen to his song.

Carter couldn't help banging out a beat on the bench with his hands as he listened.

"I didn't know teachers could sing like that," said Sara when Mr Ali had finished. "I mean, you're actually quite good!"

"And the song really gets in your head!" said Femi. "Did you just make it up?"

Mr Ali nodded and smiled as he looked at Carter.

"That's twice today I've seen your talent for a beat," he said.

Carter gave a shrug – it was what he did when he couldn't think of anything to say.

"Well, I was thinking of starting a singing club," said Mr Ali. "Would any of you be interested?"

Carter felt a flutter of excitement.

Maybe singing was something he might actually be good at?

"A singing club?" said Femi. "Like a choir?"

"I suppose so," said Mr Ali, "but we should sing the songs you all like."

Everyone thought the idea of a singing club sounded much better than a choir.

"Choirs always end up singing songs about cabbages and rainbows and stuff," said Lexi, pulling a face.

"It would mean giving up one lunchtime a week to practise," said Mr Ali.

"We don't mind," said Sara.

"What about you, Carter?" asked Mr Ali. "I get the idea you're a music fan."

Carter peered out of the window and saw Ryan was on the climbing frame with Ethan.

"Yeah, okay," Carter mumbled.

"I'll need your help to get more members," said Mr Ali. "If it goes well, we should aim to do a concert for the whole school and parents before half-term. Now *there's* an aspiration to add to your list!"

The bell rang and Mr Ali asked the children to go outside ready to line up.

"One second," Mr Ali called, waving to Carter to stay behind. "Your mum spoke to me."

Carter felt hot and awkward.

"She wanted the school to know about the difficult summer you've all had."

Difficult? Carter had mostly been bored out of his mind. Apart from when he was listening to his parents argue while his brothers cried the house down.

Mr Ali went on, "I want you to know that if you need to talk to me or any of the staff, we're here to listen and help."

Carter stared at the floor. How could talking to a teacher help him get through this?

"Right," said Mr Ali brightly. "Let's get the word out about the singing group. I have a feeling this is something you're going to be great at, Carter."

At the end of the day, Carter was surprised to see his mum and brothers waiting in the playground. Usually, he made his own way home.

"I thought we'd go for ice-creams," said Mum.

"Where's Dad?" Carter asked. His mum's red eyes told him she'd been crying.

"He's staying with Uncle Tony," she said.

"Is he coming back?" asked Carter.

Immediately he wished he hadn't asked because Mum's face crumpled. Carter helped to round up his brothers and they headed to the shop. It felt kind of normal but somehow it wasn't.

"Where's Dad's computer and guitar?" Carter demanded when they got home. The living room looked wrong. All kinds of thoughts rushed into his head. He couldn't imagine not listening to music with his dad every day. He ran upstairs and threw himself on his bed, slamming the bedroom door behind him.

3 A Surprise Soloist

The next morning, Carter was walking to school, lost in his thoughts. He was imagining himself on a stage, singing one of his dad's favourite songs. His mum and dad were in the audience, looking so proud and holding hands. Carter's daydream was interrupted when Ryan came bounding up behind him.

"My aunty says your mum and dad are splitting up," Ryan panted.

Carter flinched.

"They're not splitting up for definite," he snapped. "Dad's just gone to stay with his brother for a few days."

"That's what I mean," said Ryan, looking at Carter like he was weird. "They're splitting up."

Carter was usually happy to see Ryan. Today, he just wanted him to go away.

"Are you playing football at lunchtime?" asked Ryan.

"Maybe," said Carter. "But I might go to Mr Ali's singing club. Do you want to come?"

"Singing club!" Ryan laughed. "No way! What do you want to do that for?"

Carter didn't answer. Right now he was just glad Ryan wasn't joining the club.

When Carter got to school, he saw Lexi, Sara and Femi together in the playground.

"Hey, Carter!" called Sara. "Did you ask Ryan if he's coming to singing club?"

"He'd rather play football," Carter muttered.

"Shame," said Sara. "I've heard him sing in assembly. He's all right."

"I've asked Leon and Brianna," said Lexi. "They're definitely up for it."

Lexi walked alongside Carter as they headed into school.

"You know, my big sister Lyra breaks up with her boyfriend all the time," she said. "But they always get back together again. So, you never know, yeah?"

Yet again, Carter was stuck for words. How come everyone knew about his mum and dad breaking up?

That lunchtime, Mr Ali held his first singing club and beamed when fifteen children turned up – including Ryan.

"What are you doing here?" Carter hissed at Ryan as they waited for Mr Ali to connect his laptop to the speakers. "You laughed at me this morning when I said I was coming."

"I know," said Ryan. "But Mr Ali asked me and Sara said I had a nice voice. So I thought I'd try it."

Mr Ali started playing a backing track that Carter knew at once.

"I'd never heard *After the Storm* before Carter told me about it," Mr Ali told everyone. "But I found it online and thought it would be a brilliant song for us to try."

Carter's face went hot and he looked at the floor. This song was something he'd shared with his dad. He wasn't sure he wanted to share it with everyone at school, too.

"Cool!" said Ryan when the track finished.

Carter glanced up to see if his friend was serious.

Mr Ali went over the words with the group before inviting them to sing along.

"We sound all right," said Brianna after the first run-through.

Carter sensed that everyone really liked the song and he felt a bit lighter. It was amazing how singing helped him feel different.

Mr Ali suggested that a soloist should take the last verse, and Carter found himself raising his hand. Sara did too.

"And what about you, Ryan?" Mr Ali asked. "Would you like to give it a go?"

What! Ryan? thought Carter.

"Okay," said Ryan, looking around nervously. "If you want me to."

Carter slapped his own head. He couldn't believe it. This was his special song. When had Ryan ever been interested in music?

Mr Ali asked Ryan, Sara and Carter to sing the last verse in front of everyone.

"I know it's tough putting you on the spot," he said. "But just go for it!"

Carter and Sara took turns to sing. Sara's voice wobbled a bit but she sounded good. Then Ryan started. "It's embarrassing!" he cried. But then he got going.

"OMG, he's good," Carter heard Femi whisper.

When Ryan had finished, Lexi called out, "So, who are you going to pick to sing it?"

Mr Ali looked thoughtful.

"I'll need some time to work out what's best for the group," he said.

As the practice finished, Sara told Mr Ali she'd changed her mind about wanting to sing a solo. Mr Ali thanked her and turned to the two boys, just as Mrs Wilde popped her head around the door.

"You both sang that verse so well," said Mr Ali. "But I think it would be great for Ryan if he took on the challenge of singing the solo this time."

Ryan? Carter couldn't believe what he was hearing.

"Mr Ali, could I have a word?" Mrs Wilde called.

"Excuse me for a moment," said Mr Ali, moving swiftly to the door.

Carter couldn't hold his feelings in. "You don't even like singing!" he shouted at Ryan.

"Yes I do!" Ryan protested.

"No you don't!" shouted Carter. "You think this whole thing is silly."

"You're the silly one," said Ryan.

"Get lost!" said Carter as Ryan stormed out of the hall.

Carter glared through the window at Ryan as he stomped across the playground.

"Where's Ryan?" asked Mr Ali, returning to the room.

Carter couldn't speak. Ryan had ruined everything! Carter could have sung the solo and made his parents happy. Maybe then they'd remember how much they liked each other and everything would be all right.

"Carter, take a deep breath," said Mr Ali.

But Carter couldn't focus. All he could think about was how angry he was at Ryan.

"I'm not entirely sure what happened here," said Mr Ali calmly. "But you know, Ryan didn't come to singing club just to hurt your feelings. I encouraged him to join. He has a good voice and I think it would be good for his confidence to stand up in front of an audience."

Carter's emotions were swirling around his head like flapping, screeching birds. He wished the world would just swallow him up right now.

4 Express Yourself

Carter wasn't in the mood for lessons that afternoon. During registration he kept glancing across the room at Ryan. Part of him wanted to glare at his friend but he also wondered if he was upset after Carter had shouted at him. Ryan just kept his eyes on his book.

"Right," said Mr Ali, finishing the register. "This afternoon's lesson is on poetry."

Mr Ali could have said they were going to study the world's best footballers and Carter wouldn't have cared. But then Mr Ali started to read out some funny poems. Carter wasn't really listening to start with but when everyone started laughing, he tuned in.

Mr Ali told them how poems didn't always have to rhyme and he read out some more examples.

Carter was surprised when Mr Ali started talking about hip-hop music and how rhythm and rhyme worked together. He played some tracks by a poet and rapper called Kai Nichols. Carter felt his hands beating along.

Mr Ali explained, "The important thing with writing poetry, song lyrics or rap is to find the best way to express yourself. Focus on feelings and ideas you want to share and work out how to use words and rhythm to make someone listen to you."

He asked the class to start thinking of ideas for a poem or rap they wanted to write. Carter's mind raced. He was angry with Ryan. He was going to write those feelings down in a rap.

"You can get up and move around if it helps," Mr Ali told him, when he saw Carter jiggling his legs under the desk. Carter paced around the classroom until he'd got some ideas he could write down on paper.

At the end of the lesson, Carter couldn't wait to share his ideas with the rest of the class.

Carter found it hard to sit quietly and listen to other people's poems. Eventually, Mr Ali asked Carter to stand up and read what he'd written.

"I haven't got the whole thing done," said Carter nervously. "Just the idea of how it might start."

Carter glanced around the room and was surprised how interested most of the class looked. Ryan was looking out of the window but Sara was giving him a big grin and Lexi was doing a funny dance from her chair.

Carter started to tap his foot and play the beat in his head before he began to read.

*"After your storm of words
It's my turn to be heard ..."*

Carter paused. Mr Ali had started to clap out the beat.

"It sounds great!" Lexi cheered.

"It does," said Mr Ali. "We'll clap the beat and you rap over it. From the beginning."

Carter listened to the beat and began again.

"After your storm of words.
It's my turn to be heard.
The rage I'm feeling has to end,
After the storm it needs to mend
'cos in the end, we all know ..."

Carter looked up as the beat from the class fizzled out.

"That's as far as I got," he said quietly.

Sara and Lexi started clapping. Carter looked at Ryan. He was still staring out of the window and Carter wondered what his friend was thinking.

As they left school that afternoon, Carter was surrounded by his new friends.

Carter decided to tell them what Mr Ali had said about Ryan.

"I think Mr Ali's right," said Lexi. "Ryan wouldn't go to singing club to annoy you."

"And it would be good for Ryan to sing a solo," Femi added. "He usually hates standing up in front of people."

Carter knew they were right but he still felt a knot in his stomach when he thought about Ryan.

"Carter, you should really finish that rap," said Sara. "It sounds amazing!"

"It does," everyone agreed.

Carter shrugged but he was already thinking about how the rap could go on.

That night, Carter told his dad about singing club when he called.

"You're kidding?" Dad said down the phone. "You're performing *After the Storm*?"

"Yeah," said Carter. He paused before asking, "Will you and Mum come and watch the performance? Together?"

Dad was quiet for a few seconds.

"You know Carter, me and your mum are always going to be together when it comes to you boys. Always."

"You mean, you could get back together like things were before?" asked Carter.

"Sorry, Carter," he said. "It can't be like before. We couldn't be happy like that. What we need to do now is look out for each other. Then we can get to a new kind of normal. One that feels better for us all, okay?"

A new kind of normal? How was that possible if his dad was far away or if Carter had to

move house and school to live with him? How would Carter choose between Mum and Dad? Nothing made sense any more.

5 The Passing Storm

Over the next few weeks, Mr Ali encouraged Carter to finish his rap and to write some others, too. He usually found focusing on school work difficult, but not with this. In fact, Carter worked so hard on his songwriting that he found he was thinking about it even when he wasn't trying to. He had ideas in his head while he did all kinds of things – like having a shower or walking to school.

When he wasn't working on his rap ideas, Carter mostly talked to his new friends in the playground. Ryan was usually playing football over on the field. They'd hardly spoken since their argument and Carter just looked down whenever Ryan came near.

There were just two days left before the start of the half-term break and the singing group's performance was tomorrow. Mr Ali caught Carter by the classroom door just before he headed out for his lunch.

"I wonder if it's time you started talking to Ryan again," Mr Ali said.

Carter sighed and looked away.

"It would be good to see you two patch things up," Mr Ali added. "I have a feeling that's partly what you've been writing about. Why don't you give it a try?"

Carter saw Ryan in the lunch queue and wondered if Mr Ali had spoken to him, too. Then Ryan came and put his tray down in the place opposite Carter.

"Hey," said Ryan, sitting down.

Carter barely looked up. "Hey."

"Um ... How are you feeling about the concert?" asked Ryan.

"Okay," Carter mumbled.

"I'm totally freaked!" said Ryan. "I keep thinking I'm going to mess up my solo. Just thinking about it is making my head hurt."

Carter knew that singing a solo was a big deal for anyone – but especially for Ryan.

"You always sound great," said Carter, staring at his plate.

"Yeah?" said Ryan. "Really?"

Carter took a deep breath and felt the knot in his stomach untwist a bit.

"Yeah," Carter said. He forced his head up to look his friend in the face. "And we'll all be standing there with you."

Ryan's face broke into a smile. "Thanks, Carter! You're really into music so, you know, what you think matters," he said. He dived into his lunch and then looked up. "Are you going to eat those chips?" he asked, glancing at Carter's plate.

Carter grinned. "Just watch me," he said, suddenly feeling hungry.

The next morning, Carter looked out for Ryan on his way to school. He'd missed joking around with him. And it wasn't just the concert Carter wanted to talk about. Last night on the phone his dad had said he was looking at flats.

He'd told Carter that there would be room for him and his brothers there, but how was it going to work? Then Carter had reminded Dad about the concert and he had just wished him luck and couldn't say for sure if he could come.

But there was no sign of Ryan on the walk to school that morning. When Carter got to the classroom, he wasn't there either. Nor was Mr Ali. The room was buzzing as everyone talked about the concert and how nervous they were feeling.

Finally, Mr Ali came in. He held up his hand and the class fell silent.

"Bad news I'm afraid," he said, frowning. "Ryan's sick."

6 The Concert

Carter stared at Mr Ali. How could this happen after he'd been laughing with Ryan just the day before? Then he remembered how stressed Ryan had been and how he'd said his head was hurting. Was that why Ryan was off sick?

"But what about Ryan's solo?" Lexi called out.

Everyone started talking at once and Mr Ali held up his hand.

"Does anyone else feel confident taking the solo?" he asked, looking around the room. Everyone shrank in their seats. "We could squeeze in a practice before the concert."

"No way!" groaned Brianna. "Nobody sings like Ryan."

Mr Ali looked around the room and sighed.

"What about Carter's rap?" said Femi quietly.

"What did you say?" asked Sara.

Femi squirmed as all eyes turned to him but he looked at Mr Ali and spoke more loudly. "Couldn't Carter perform his rap instead?"

Carter's stomach did a flip and he stared at Femi with wide eyes.

"Carter, what do you think?" Mr Ali asked.

Carter looked around the room and scratched his head. All his friends were looking at him.

"All right," he said, feeling a small smile creep across his face. He'd have a chance to make his parents happy after all!

Before Carter knew it, the singing group met in the hall, ready for the concert. Carter's feet and knees were vibrating so much the whole bench was shaking.

"You're going to be great," Lexi whispered into his ear.

Sara's dad came in at the back and Sara looked surprised but happy. A few weeks ago, Carter hadn't been sure he'd get on with Sara, but now they were becoming friends.

At the last moment, Carter's mum came into the hall. Carter's heartbeat skidded. Where was his dad? A hush fell over the crowd as Mrs Wilde stood up, ready to start the concert.

No, no, no! Carter couldn't breathe and his head started pounding. He couldn't perform if his dad wasn't there.

He looked at his mum. She was also scanning the rows of adults at the back, looking for his dad.

Mrs Wilde welcomed the visitors and made some announcements as Carter forced back tears and tried to swallow the lump in his throat. He had to get a grip, or he'd never be able to rap.

Mr Ali started playing the backing track. Carter felt Lexi's hand yanking him up as the rest of the group stood. They were supposed to stand up quietly but they didn't. Femi almost fell off the stage but Brianna grabbed him just in time.

Carter looked across to Mr Ali and waved his hands to show he couldn't do it.

He needed everything to stop. Mr Ali looked confused. Then the door banged at the back of the hall.

"Look!" hissed Lexi.

Carter turned and saw his dad standing in the doorway, bent over and panting.

As Carter's dad gave him a thumbs up, the singing group made their worst start to singing their song – ever! Mr Ali stopped the track.

"Whoops!" he said. "Let's try again."

Everyone laughed and Carter felt the lump in his throat start to melt away.

The group started the song again and this time they sounded great. Bar by bar and note by note, Carter felt his heart pounding hard. What would he sound like when he started to rap?

Would he forget the words? Would everyone laugh? What would his mum and dad think? He had to make them see that they needed to stay together.

It was almost the end of the concert and time for his rap. Carter's legs shook as the singing group began clapping the beat for him. He wasn't sure how he did it, but his voice started loudly filling the silent hall. He could hardly believe how powerful he felt. He saw his mum and dad's faces looking at him with such pride and Carter felt like he was flying. He couldn't stop grinning as the last line of his rap rang out.

It was the end of the concert and the audience burst into applause. Many people stood up – including Carter's mum and dad. Mrs Wilde invited the children to take a bow, then asked Carter to step up to the front of the stage.

"I think you'll all agree that Carter really let his talents shine today," she said.

Everyone gave Carter a huge extra clap and the singing group whooped and cheered. Carter looked back at his friends and grinned.

The singing group sat down while Mrs Wilde made some announcements and gave out certificates. By the time she'd finished, the whole school was wriggling around so much, they looked like they were sitting on top of an ants' nest.

Carter was happy to go and collect his things for home time.

"Do you want to play football down the park later?" Lexi asked, as they headed outside.

"It depends if Dad's coming back to ours," Carter said. Then all sorts of scary questions rushed back into his head.

"Okay!" said Lexi. "Maybe see you later."

Carter smiled when he saw his mum and dad standing together in the playground. Had his plan worked?

"Did you really write that rap?" asked Dad, beaming. Carter nodded.

"And you performed it so well!" said Mum. "We're so proud of you."

"I've sorted my new flat," said Dad.

Carter suddenly felt sick. Was he going to have to leave Greenwicks and his new friends, just when things were starting to feel okay again?

"It's just a few streets away from you all," said Dad.

"You and the boys will live with me," said Mum. "But you can stay at your dad's any time you like. We're working things out."

Carter stared at his parents and the sick feeling vanished. He wouldn't have to choose between his parents after all.

"What were the words in your rap?" his dad asked as they headed out of the playground. "I really liked them. Something about after all the fighting …"

Carter knew the bit his dad meant.

"After the storm and the pain of the fight,
I know that everything will be alright,"
said Carter.

"Yeah," said Dad. "That feels about right to
me. You're really talented, Carter."

Carter smiled. "Thanks, Dad."

"Hey, I heard this great new song last night,"
said Dad. "Do you want to listen to it when
we get to your mum's?"

Carter grinned and nodded. Then, with
his mum and dad each side of him, they
made their way home together, chatting
and laughing.

Chat about the book

1   Go to the final chapter. Why didn't Carter want the concert to begin?

2   Read page 11. Why was Carter expecting to be told off?

3   Read page 47. Which word tells you that Femi is uncomfortable when everyone turns to look at him?

4   Why is chapter 3 called, *'The Surprise Soloist'*?

5   Go to page 37. Why was Ryan looking out of the window?

6   Go to Chapter 2. Why did a singing club sound a better idea than a choir to the children?

7   Do you think Ryan and Carter will remain friends after Year 6? Give reasons for and against.

8   What qualities did Mr Ali have as a teacher? Which qualities do you think are important to have as a teacher?